SAY IT WITH ZEST

By Mindy Shapiro
Illustrated by Aaron Friedman

Some people speak English
Some speak Japanese.

Some people speak Persian.
Some speak Portuguese.

Whatever the twists
Your tongue learned to take
Whatever the shapes
Your lips learned to make,

There's one thing that's certain
No one can deny:

"What a beautiful picture!"
"Your baby is sweet."

"That's a marvelous haircut."
"Your room is so neat."

"Your lunch smells delicious."
"Your mother's so kind."

"You're the most splendid pal
I ever could find."

lovely
fantastic
adorable

The list is quite long.
Full of good things, galore
Waiting to be said.

"Please pass the butter."
"Thanks for the ride."

"Excuse me, but could you
Please step aside."

"We missed you last week."
"What a home run!"

"Rebbe, in your class
Learning is fun."

If a new neighbor moved in
Hmm ... What could you say?

"Come over and visit.
Come over to play."

Saying nice things is simple
It's easy to do

Put on a smile
And look for your cue.

"Mom, you're the best
cook in the East.
This meal you prepared
was quite some feast."

"Bubby and Zaidy
Wow! We're delighted
We love when you visit
We're downright excited."

Your tongue and your lips
Have got magical might.

They take upside down smiles
And turn them upright.

No nice things to say?

Give your tongue a rest.